Unicorn Sleepover

Maverick
Early Readers

'Unicorn Sleepover'
An original concept by Alison Donald
© Alison Donald

Illustrated by Erin Brown

Published by MAVERICK ARTS PUBLISHING LTD
Studio 11, City Business Centre, 6 Brighton Road,
Horsham, West Sussex, RH13 5BB
© Maverick Arts Publishing Limited November 2020
+44 (0)1403 256941

A CIP catalogue record for this book is available at the British Library.

ISBN 978-1-84886-715-4

www.maverickbooks.co.uk

This book is rated as: Purple Band (Guided Reading)

Unicorn Sleepover

By **Alison Donald**
Illustrated by **Erin Brown**

Naz had always loved unicorns. She wished more than anything that she could ride one. Luckily for Naz, she saw a competition on a cereal box:

'Find a token inside to win a Unicorn Sleepover!'

Naz had finally won a Unicorn Sleepover.

"I'm going to ride a real live unicorn!" Naz cried.

"And I'm going to eat cereal forever," Naz's

mum sighed.

Hartford Farm was on top of a green hill.

The sign said, '**Hartford Farm - Where**

Dreams Come True'.

Naz wasn't the only winner. There were other

girls there, and boys too.

"Hello everyone! I'm Cindy, your camp

counsellor. Let's get started on our sleepover!"

The fairy lights in the girls' bedroom sparkled and glowed. Everyone got changed into unicorn pyjamas. They ate popcorn in their beds and watched a unicorn movie. Naz even had a pillow fight! She was having the best time ever, but she was desperate to meet her unicorn.

"Cindy," said Naz, "when will we get to meet the unicorns?"

"Soon." Cindy smiled.

Next, it was time for stories around a campfire. The children had fun with their torches.

Naz loved toasting marshmallows, but she couldn't stop thinking about unicorns.

"Cindy, is it time to meet the unicorns now?"
"Be patient," Cindy said with a smile.

Naz smiled back, but it was just so hard waiting!

Then it was time for a late-night feast!

There were 'ooh's and 'ahh's from the children.

Naz had never seen a giant unicorn chocolate

fountain before!

But she just couldn't stop thinking about the

real unicorns.

"Please can we meet our unicorns now?"

Naz asked.

Cindy smiled. "It's getting late. I promise

you will meet them in the morning."

Naz sighed.

Everyone got into their beds. It had been the

best night ever. Naz eventually drifted off to

sleep and dreamed of meeting her unicorn.

Naz's eyes popped open – the sun was shining!

Hooray! It was morning.

"It's time to meet the unicorns," Cindy

announced.

Everyone cheered. Naz and the others got

dressed and ran over to the stables.

Cindy called out a list of names. "Naz, you're with Sprinkles," she said.

But something wasn't right. Sprinkles was brown. She was small and stocky. Her hair was short and coarse. And her horn...

Her horn was attached by a strap!

"This isn't a real unicorn!" Naz cried.

Her eyes welled up with tears.

Naz turned and ran back to the bedroom.

"Naz, are you ok?" Cindy asked, peering round the door.

"I thought there would be real unicorns," Naz cried.

"I'm sorry, Naz. Unicorns are rare and magical. I'm sure we'll meet one someday. But in the meantime, Sprinkles is a very special pony. She likes children and she needs lots of love."

Naz wiped her tears away. She couldn't believe she had opened twenty boxes of cereal for THIS! "Maybe you'll feel better once you spend some time with Sprinkles," said Cindy.

Naz wasn't sure about that.

Next, everyone gathered to muck out the ponies.

"What does 'muck out' mean?" a girl asked.

"It means we have to shovel poo," Naz grumbled.

Naz was still unhappy about being paired up with a pony. Naz shovelled the poo and heaped it into piles.

"This is so gross," she moaned.

Then, she slipped and fell into one of the piles.

Could this day get any worse?

Then it was time to feed the ponies.

Naz forgot to keep her hand flat and the pony

nibbled on her finger.

"OW!" she yelled.

This was no fun at all.

"Grab your brushes everyone," said Cindy.

"It's time to brush."

Sprinkles closed her eyes and sighed as Naz brushed her. Naz sighed too. Brushing was much

better than shovelling and feeding.

Sprinkles looked up with her big brown eyes.

Naz looked at Sprinkles properly for the first time. Sprinkles looked so kind, so trusting.

Naz rubbed her nose, and then Sprinkles did something unexpected. She rested her head on Naz's shoulder. Naz couldn't help but smile.

"Looks like you've made a friend!" said Cindy.

Naz had to admit that Sprinkles was quite sweet -

for a pony.

"Now for the best part. It's time to go for a ride."

Soon Naz was sitting on Sprinkles's back.

Naz felt the wind in her hair and the warm

sun on her face.

"Wow, Sprinkles! We're actually riding!"

It was the best feeling in the world.

For a moment, Naz forgot all about unicorns.

"Good girl, Sprinkles." She patted Sprinkles's
neck.

Naz's mum was waiting back at the barn.

"So, how was the sleepover, sweetheart?"

There was so much to say, Naz didn't know where to start. "It wasn't what I expected... but I'm so glad I came!"

Sprinkles put her head on Naz's shoulder and this time, Naz gave her a hug.

"Great job looking after Sprinkles," said Cindy.

"Would you like to come back sometime and help

take care of her?"

Naz grinned. "That would be great! Thank you!"

There were no unicorns at Hartford Farm.

But it truly was a magical place.

"Bye Sprinkles! See you soon," Naz waved.

Quiz

1. Where does Naz see the competition to win a Unicorn Sleepover?
a) On a cereal box
b) On TV
c) In a book

2. Where is Hartford Farm?
a) In the city
b) Underground
c) On top of a green hill

3. What do the unicorns turn out to be?
a) Zebras
b) Ponies
c) Donkeys

4. What does Sprinkles nibble?

a) Carrots

b) Naz's finger

c) A hairbrush

5. What does Naz get to do at the end of the day?

a) Ride Sprinkles

b) Eat more cereal

c) Muck out the ponies

Book Bands for Guided Reading

The Institute of Education book banding system is a scale of colours that reflects the various levels of reading difficulty. The bands are assigned by taking into account the content, the language style, the layout and phonics. Word, phrase and sentence level work is also taken into consideration.

Maverick Early Readers are a bright, attractive range of books covering the pink to white bands. All of these books have been book banded for guided reading to the industry standard and edited by a leading educational consultant.

Pink
Red
Yellow
Blue
Green
Orange
Turquoise
Purple
Gold
White

To view the whole Maverick Readers scheme, visit our website at
www.maverickearlyreaders.com

Or scan the QR code above to view our scheme instantly!

Quiz Answers: 1a, 2c, 3b, 4b, 5a